LOOK

MICHAEL GREJNIEC

NORTH-SOUTH BOOKS / NEW YORK

Published in the United States by North-South Books Inc., New York.

Published simultaneously in Great Britain, Canada,
Australia, and New Zealand in 1993 by North-South Books,
an imprint of Nord-Süd Verlag AG, Gossau Zürich, Switzerland.

Library of Congress Cataloging in Publication Data
Grejniec, Michael.
Look / Michael Grejniec.
Summary: Bored with being sick in bed, a child looks out
his window and finds the street full of interesting people and activities.
ISBN 1-55858-212-6 (trade binding)
ISBN 1-55858-213-4 (library binding)
[1. Neighborhood—Fiction. 2. Sick—Fiction.] I. Title.
PZ7.G8625Lo 1993
[E]—dc20 93-16066

British Library Cataloguing in Publication Data
Grejniec, Michael
Look
I. Title
823
ISBN 1-55858-212-6

1 3 5 7 9 10 8 6 4 2
Printed in Belgium

The art was painted with Holbein watercolors
on Colombe paper. The color separations
were made from transparencies.

Book design by Michael Grejniec

I'm sick.
The doctor says I have to
stay in bed all day. There's nothing
to do but stare out of the window.
How boring.

Look, there's the doctor going away.
No one is awake yet.
Do you hear a funny noise?

Look, it was a plane.
See the shadow moving
across the building?
And there's my friend Marc.
His mother is making his lunch.

Look, a woman is feeding her bird.
Now people are waking up.
Where is that man going with all
those cans of paint?

Look, the cat's sneaking
out of the front door.
I wish I could go to school today.

Look, some birds have landed
on the windowsill. I wonder what
they're talking about.
It's getting warm outside.

Look, Marc's mother is hanging
the clothes out to dry.
Why is the cat running away?

Look, a man is getting ready
to play the saxophone.
And there's Miss Kellett with the mail.
I wonder if she will bring me
a letter from Grandmother.

Look, the little bird's flying away!

Look, the woman is so sad.
I hope the bird will come back.

Look, something strange is coming.
Do you hear that music?

Look, the circus is in town!
I wish I could go outside.

Look, the monkey is playing the drums.
What a show!
I'm starting to feel better already.

Look, the juggler is giving
the balls to all my friends.
They're lucky!

Look, Marc's sister is waving at me!

"We brought you a ball from the juggler.
    We thought you might be bored."
"Thanks, but I'm not bored at all.
    Come here and look out of my window!"

E
GRE

Grejniec, Michael.

Look.

$14.95

DATE			